William Tell Told Again

P. G. Wodehouse

Illustrations: Philip Dadd
Described In Verse: John W. Houghton

The Manor Wodehouse Collection

TARK CLASSIC FICTION

JAN 1 5 2013

AN IMPRINT OF

ARC
MANOR
Rockville, Maryland
2008

ISBN: 978-1-60450-045-5

Published by TARK Classic Fiction
An Imprint of Arc Manor
P. O. Box 10339
Rockville, MD 20849-0339
www.ArcManor.com

Printed in the United States of America/United Kingdom

To Biddy O'Sullivan
for a Christmas Present

The Swiss, against their Austrian foes,
Had ne'er a soul to lead 'em,
Till Tell, as you've heard tell, arose
And guided them to freedom.
Tell's tale we tell again – an act
For which pray no one scold us—
This tale of Tell we tell, in fact,
As this Tell tale was told us.

William Tell Told Again

Please Visit

www.ManorWodehouse.com

for a complete list of titles available in our
Manor Wodehouse Collection

CHAPTER 1

ONCE upon a time, more years ago than anybody can remember, before the first hotel had been built or the first Englishman had taken a photograph of Mont Blanc and brought it home to be pasted in an album and shown after tea to his envious friends, Switzerland belonged to the Emperor of Austria, to do what he liked with.

One of the first things the Emperor did was to send his friend Hermann Gessler to govern the country. Gessler was not a nice man, and it soon became plain that he would never make himself really popular with the Swiss. The point on which they disagreed in particular was the question of taxes. The Swiss, who were a simple and thrifty people, objected to paying taxes of any sort. They said they wanted to spend their money on all kinds of other things. Gessler, on the other hand, wished to put a tax on everything, and, being Governor, he did it. He made everyone who owned a flock of sheep pay a certain sum of money to him; and if the farmer sold his sheep and bought cows, he had to pay rather more money to Gessler for the cows than he had paid for the sheep. Gessler also taxed bread, and biscuits, and jam, and buns, and lemonade, and, in fact, everything he could think of, till the people of Switzerland determined to complain. They appointed Walter Furst, who had red hair and looked fierce; Werner Stauffacher, who had gray hair and was always wondering how he ought to pronounce his name; and Arnold of Melchthal, who had light-yellow hair and was supposed to know a great deal about the law, to make the complaint. They called on the Governor one lovely morning in April, and were shown into the Hall of Audience.

"Well," said Gessler, "and what's the matter now?"

The other two pushed Walter Furst forward because he looked fierce, and they thought he might frighten the Governor.

Walter Furst coughed.

"Well?" asked Gessler.

"Er – ahem!" said Walter Furst.

"That's the way," whispered Werner; "*give* it him!"

"Er – ahem!" said Walter Furst again; "the fact is, your Governorship – "

"It's a small point," interrupted Gessler, "but I'm generally called 'your Excellency.' Yes?"

"The fact is, your Excellency, it seems to the people of Switzerland – "

" – Whom I represent," whispered Arnold of Melchthal.

" – Whom I represent, that things want changing."

"What things?" inquired Gessler.

"The taxes, your excellent Governorship."

"Change the taxes? Why, don't the people of Switzerland think there are enough taxes?"

Arnold of Melchthal broke in hastily.

"They think there are many too many," he said. "What with the tax on sheep, and the tax on cows, and the tax on bread, and the tax on tea, and the tax – "

"I know, *I* know," Gessler interrupted; "I know all the taxes. Come to the point. What about 'em?"

"Well, your Excellency, there are too many of them."

"Too many!"

"Yes. And we are not going to put up with it any longer!" shouted Arnold of Melchthal.

Gessler leaned forward in his throne.

"Might I ask you to repeat that remark?" he said.

"We are not going to put up with it any longer!"

Gessler sat back again with an ugly smile.

"Oh," he said – "oh, indeed! You aren't, aren't you! Desire the Lord High Executioner to step this way," he added to a soldier who stood beside him.

The Lord High Executioner entered the presence. He was a kind-looking old gentleman with white hair, and he wore a beautiful black robe, tastefully decorated with death's-heads.

"Your Excellency sent for me?" he said.

"Just so," replied Gessler. "This gentleman here" – he pointed to Arnold of Melchthal – "says he does not like taxes, and that he isn't going to put up with them any longer."

"Tut-tut!" murmured the executioner.

"See what you can do for him."

"Certainly, your Excellency. Robert," he cried, "is the oil on the boil?"

"Just this minute boiled over," replied a voice from the other side of the door.

"Then bring it in, and mind you don't spill any."

Enter Robert, in a suit of armour and a black mask, carrying a large caldron, from which the steam rose in great clouds.

"Now, sir, if you please," said the executioner politely to Arnold of Melchthal.

Arnold looked at the caldron.

"Why, it's hot," he said.

"Warmish," admitted the executioner.

"It's against the law to threaten a man with hot oil."

"You may bring an action against me," said the executioner. "Now, sir, if *you* please. We are wasting time. The forefinger of your left hand, if I may trouble you. Thank you. I am obliged."

He took Arnold's left hand, and dipped the tip of the first finger into the oil.

"Ow!" cried Arnold, jumping.

"Don't let him see he's hurting you," whispered Werner Stauffacher. "Pretend you don't notice it."

Gessler leaned forward again.

"Have your views on taxes changed at all?" he asked. "Do you see my point of view more clearly now?"

Arnold admitted that he thought that, after all, there might be something to be said for it.

"That's right," said the Governor. "And the tax on sheep? You don't object to that?"

"No."

"And the tax on cows?"

"I like it."

"And those on bread, and buns, and lemonade?"

"I enjoy them."

"Excellent. In fact, you're quite contented?"

"Quite."

"And you think the rest of the people are?"

"Oh, quite, quite!"

"And do you think the same?" he asked of Walter and Werner.

"Oh *yes*, your Excellency!" they cried.

"Then *that's* all right," said Gessler. "I was sure you would be sensible about it. Now, if you will kindly place in the tambourine which the gentleman on my left is presenting to you a mere trifle to compensate us for our trouble in giving you an audience, and if you" (to Arnold of Melchthal) "will contribute an additional trifle for use of the Imperial boiling oil, I think we shall all be satisfied. You've done it? *That's* right. Good-bye, and mind the step as you go out."

And, as he finished this speech, the three spokesmen of the people of Switzerland were shown out of the Hall of Audience.

CHAPTER 2

THEY were met in the street outside by a large body of their fellow-citizens, who had accompanied them to the Palace, and who had been spending the time since their departure in listening by turns at the keyhole of the front-door. But as the Hall of Audience was at the other side of the Palace, and cut off from the front-door by two other doors, a flight of stairs, and a long passage, they had not heard very much of what had gone on inside, and they surrounded the three spokesmen as they came out, and questioned them eagerly.

"Has he taken off the tax on jam?" asked Ulric the smith.

"What is he going to do about the tax on mixed biscuits?" shouted Klaus von der Flue, who was a chimney-sweep of the town and loved mixed biscuits.

"Never mind about tea and mixed biscuits!" cried his neighbour, Meier of Sarnen. "What I want to know is whether we shall have to pay for keeping sheep any more."

"What *did* the Governor say?" asked Jost Weiler, a practical man, who liked to go straight to the point.

The three spokesmen looked at one another a little doubtfully.

"We-e-ll," said Werner Stauffacher at last, "as a matter of fact, he didn't actually *say* very much. It was more what he *did*, if you understand me, than what he said."

"I should describe His Excellency the Governor," said Walter Furst, "as a man who has got a way with him – a man who has got all sorts of arguments at his finger-tips."

At the mention of finger-tips, Arnold of Melchthal uttered a sharp howl.

"In short," continued Walter, "after a few minutes' very interesting conversation he made us see that it really wouldn't do, and that we must go on paying the taxes as before."

There was a dead silence for several minutes, while everybody looked at everybody else in dismay.

The silence was broken by Arnold of Sewa. Arnold of Sewa had been disappointed at not being chosen as one of the three spokesmen, and he thought that if he had been so chosen all this trouble would not have occurred.

"The fact is," he said bitterly, "that you three have failed to do what you were sent to do. I mention no names – far from it – but I don't mind saying that there are some people in this town who would have given a better account of themselves. What you want in little matters of this sort is, if I may say so, tact. Tact; that's what you want. Of course, if you *will* go rushing into the Governor's presence – "

"But we didn't rush," said Walter Furst.

" – Shouting out that you want the taxes abolished – "

"But we didn't shout," said Walter Furst.

"I really cannot speak if I am to be constantly interrupted," said Arnold of Sewa severely. "What I say is, that you ought to employ tact. Tact; that's what you want. If I had been chosen to represent the Swiss people in this affair – I am not saying I ought to have been, mind you; I merely say *if* I had been – I should have acted rather after the following fashion: Walking firmly, but not defiantly, into the tyrant's presence, I should have broken the ice with some pleasant remark about the weather. The conversation once started, the rest would have been easy. I should have said that I hoped His Excellency had enjoyed a good dinner. Once on the subject of food, and it would have been the simplest of tasks to show him how unnecessary taxes on food were, and the whole affair would have been pleasantly settled while you waited. I do not imply that the Swiss people would have done better to have chosen me as their representative. I merely say that that is how I should have acted had they done so."

And Arnold of Sewa twirled his moustache and looked offended. His friends instantly suggested that he should be allowed to try where the other three had failed, and the rest of the crowd, beginning to hope once more, took up the cry. The result was that the visitors' bell of the Palace was rung for the second time. Arnold of Sewa went in, and the door was banged behind him.

Five minutes later he came out, sucking the first finger of his left hand.

"No," he said; "it can't be done. The tyrant has convinced me."

"I knew he would," said Arnold of Melchthal.

"Then I think you might have warned me," snapped Arnold of Sewa, dancing with the pain of his burnt finger.

"Was it hot?"

"Boiling."

"Ah!"

"Then he really won't let us off the taxes?" asked the crowd in disappointed voices.

"No."

"Then the long and short of it is," said Walter Furst, drawing a deep breath, "that we must rebel!"

"Rebel?" cried everybody.

"Rebel!" repeated Walter firmly.

"We will!" cried everybody.

"Down with the tyrant!" shouted Walter Furst.

"Down with the taxes!" shrieked the crowd.

A scene of great enthusiasm followed. The last words were spoken by Werner Stauffacher.

"We want a leader," he said.

"I don't wish to thrust myself forward," began Arnold of Sewa, "but I must say, if it comes to leading – "

"And I know the very man for the job," said Werner Stauffacher. "William Tell!"

"Hurrah for William Tell!" roared the crowd, and, taking the time from Werner Stauffacher, they burst into the grand old Swiss chant which runs as follows:

> *"For he's a jolly good fellow!*
> *For he's a jolly good fellow!!*
> *For he's a jolly good fe-e-ll-ow!!!!*
> *And so say all of us!"*

And having sung this till they were all quite hoarse, they went off to their beds to get a few hours' sleep before beginning the labours of the day.

CHAPTER 3

IN a picturesque little chalet high up in the mountains, covered with snow and edelweiss (which is a flower that grows in the Alps, and you are not allowed to pick it), dwelt William Tell, his wife Hedwig, and his two sons, Walter and William. Such a remarkable man was Tell that I think I must devote a whole chapter to him and his exploits. There was really nothing he could not do. He was the best shot with the cross-bow in the whole of Switzerland. He had the courage of a lion, the sure-footedness of a wild goat, the agility of a squirrel, and a beautiful beard. If you wanted someone to hurry across desolate ice-fields, and leap from crag to crag after a chamois, Tell was the man for your money. If you wanted a man to say rude things to the Governor, it was to Tell that you applied first. Once when he was hunting in the wild ravine of Schachenthal, where men were hardly ever to be seen, he met the Governor face to face. There was no way of getting past. On one side the rocky wall rose sheer up, while below the river roared. Directly Gessler caught sight of Tell striding along with his cross-bow, his cheeks grew pale and his knees tottered, and he sat down on a rock feeling very unwell indeed.

"Aha!" said Tell. "Oho! so it's you, is it? *I* know you. And a nice sort of person you are, with your taxes on bread and sheep, aren't you! You'll come to a bad end one of these days, that's what will happen to you. Oh, you old reprobate! Pooh!" And he had passed on with a look of scorn, leaving Gessler to think over what he had said. And Gessler ever since had had a grudge against him, and was only waiting for a chance of paying him out.

"Mark my words," said Tell's wife, Hedwig, when her husband told her about it after supper that night – "mark my words, he will never forgive you."

"I will avoid him," said Tell. "He will not seek me."

"Well, mind you do," was Hedwig's reply.

On another occasion, when the Governor's soldiers were chasing a friend of his, called Baumgarten, and when Baumgarten's only chance of escape was to cross the lake during a fierce storm, and when the ferryman, sensibly remarking, "What! must I rush into the jaws of death? No man that hath his senses would do that!" refused to take out his boat even for twice his proper fare, and when the soldiers rode down to seize their prey with dreadful shouts, Tell jumped into the boat, and, rowing with all his might, brought his friend safe across after a choppy passage. Which made Gessler the Governor still more angry with him.

But it was as a marksman that Tell was so extraordinary. There was nobody in the whole of the land who was half so skilful. He attended every meeting for miles around where there was a shooting competition, and every time he won first prize. Even his rivals could not help praising his skill. "Behold!" they would say, "Tell is quite the pot-hunter," meaning by the last word a man who always went in for every prize, and always won it. And Tell would say, "Yes, truly am I a pot-hunter, for I hunt to fill the family pot." And so he did. He never came home empty-handed from the chase. Sometimes it was a chamois that he brought back, and then the family had it roasted on the first day, cold on the next four, and minced on the sixth, with sippets of toast round the edge of the dish. Sometimes it was only

a bird (as on the cover of this book), and then Hedwig would say, "Mark my words, this fowl will not go round." But it always did, and it never happened that there was not even a fowl to eat.

In fact, Tell and his family lived a very happy, contented life, in spite of the Governor Gessler and his taxes.

Tell was very patriotic. He always believed that some day the Swiss would rise and rebel against the tyranny of the Governor, and he used to drill his two children so as to keep them always in a state of preparation. They would march about, beating tin cans and shouting, and altogether enjoying themselves immensely, though Hedwig, who did not like noise, and wanted Walter and William to help her with the housework, made frequent complaints. "Mark my words," she would say, "this growing spirit of militarism in the young and foolish will lead to no good," meaning that boys who played at soldiers instead of helping their mother to dust the chairs and scrub the kitchen floor would in all probability come to a bad end. But Tell would say, "Who hopes to fight his way through life must be prepared to wield arms. Carry on, my boys!" And they carried on. It was to this man that the Swiss people had determined to come for help.

CHAPTER 4

TALKING matters over in the inn of the town, the Glass and Glacier, the citizens came to the conclusion that they ought to appoint three spokesmen to go and explain to Tell just what they wanted him to do.

"I don't wish to seem to boast at all," said Arnold of Sewa, "but I think I had better be one of the three."

"I was thinking," said Werner Stauffacher, "that it would be a pity always to be chopping and changing. Why not choose the same three as were sent to Gessler?"

"I don't desire to be unpleasant at all," replied Arnold of Sewa, "but I must be forgiven for reminding the honourable gentleman who has just spoken that he and his equally honourable friends did not meet with the best of success when they called upon the Governor."

"Well, and you didn't either!" snapped Arnold of Melchthal, whose finger still hurt him, and made him a little bad-tempered.

"That," said Arnold of Sewa, "I put down entirely to the fact that you and your friends, by not exercising tact, irritated the Governor, and made him unwilling to listen to anybody else. Nothing is more important in these affairs than tact. That's what you want – tact. But have it your own way. Don't mind *me!*"

And the citizens did not. They chose Werner Stauffacher, Arnold of Melchthal, and Walter Furst, and, having drained their glasses, the three trudged up the steep hill which led to Tell's house.

It had been agreed that everyone should wait at the Glass and Glacier until the three spokesmen returned, in order that they might hear the result of their mission. Everybody was very anxious. A revolution without Tell would be quite impossible, and it was not unlikely that Tell might refuse to be their leader. The worst of a revolution is that, if it fails, the leader is always executed as an example to the rest. And many people object to being executed, however much it may set a good example to their friends. On the other hand, Tell was a brave man and a patriot, and might be only too eager to try to throw off the tyrant's yoke, whatever the risk. They had waited about an hour, when they saw the three spokesmen coming down the hill. Tell was not with them, a fact which made the citizens suspect that he had refused their offer. The first thing a man does when he has accepted the leadership of a revolution is to come and plot with his companions.

"Well?" said everybody eagerly, as the three arrived.

Werner Stauffacher shook his head.

"Ah," said Arnold of Sewa, "I see what it is. He has refused. You didn't exercise tact, and he refused."

"We *did* exercise tact," said Stauffacher indignantly; "but he would not be persuaded. It was like this: We went to the house and knocked at the door. Tell opened it. 'Good-morning,' I said.

"'Good-morning,' said he. 'Take a seat.'

"I took a seat.

"'My heart is full,' I said, 'and longs to speak with you.' I thought that a neat way of putting it."

The company murmured approval.

"'A heavy heart,' said Tell, 'will not grow light with words.'"

"Not bad that!" murmured Jost Weiler. "Clever way of putting things, Tell has got."

"'Yet words,' I said, 'might lead us on to deeds.'"

"Neat," said Jost Weiler – "very neat. Yes?"

"To which Tell's extraordinary reply was: 'The only thing to do is to sit still.'

"'What!' I said; 'bear in silence things unbearable?'

"'Yes,' said Tell; 'to peaceable men peace is gladly granted. When the Governor finds that his oppression does not make us revolt, he will grow tired of oppressing.'"

"And what did you say to that?" asked Ulric the smith.

"I said he did not know the Governor if he thought he could ever grow tired of oppressing. 'We might do much,' I said, 'if we held fast together. Union is strength,' I said.

"'The strong,' said Tell, 'is strongest when he stands alone.'

"'Then our country must not count on thee,' I said, 'when in despair she stands on self-defence?'

"'Oh, well,' he said, 'hardly that, perhaps. I don't want to desert you. What I mean to say is, I'm no use as a plotter or a counsellor and that sort of thing. Where I come out strong is in deeds. So don't invite me to your meetings and make me speak, and that sort of thing; but if you want a man to *do* anything – why, that's where I shall come in, you see. Just write if you want me – a postcard will do – and you will not find William Tell hanging back. No, sir.' And with those words he showed us out."

"Well," said Jost Weiler, "I call that encouraging. All we have to do now is to plot. Let us plot."

"Yes, let's!" shouted everybody.

Ulric the smith rapped for silence on the table.

"Gentlemen," he said, "our friend Mr. Klaus von der Flue will now read a paper on 'Governors – their drawbacks, and how to get rid of them.' Silence, gentlemen, please. Now, then, Klaus, old fellow, speak up and get it over."

And the citizens settled down without further delay to a little serious plotting.

Chapter 5

A few days after this, Hedwig gave Tell a good talking to on the subject of his love for adventure. He was sitting at the door of his house mending an axe. Hedwig, as usual, was washing up. Walter and William were playing with a little cross-bow not far off.

"Father," said Walter.

"Yes, my boy?"

"My bow-string has bust." ("Bust" was what all Swiss boys said when they meant "broken.")

"You must mend it yourself, my boy," said Tell. "A sportsman always helps himself."

"What *I* say," said Hedwig, bustling out of the house, "is that a boy of his age has no business to be shooting. I don't like it."

"Nobody can shoot well if he does not begin to practise early. Why, when I was a boy – I remember on one occasion, when – "

"What *I* say," interrupted Hedwig, "is that a boy ought not to want always to be shooting, and what not. He ought to stay at home and help his mother. And I wish you would set them a better example."

"Well, the fact is, you know," said Tell, "I don't think Nature meant me to be a stay-at-home and that sort of thing. I couldn't be a herdsman if you paid me. I shouldn't know what to do. No; everyone has his special line, and mine is hunting. Now, I *can* hunt."

"A nasty, dangerous occupation," said Hedwig. "I don't like to hear of your being lost on desolate ice-fields, and leaping from crag to crag, and what not. Some day, mark my words, if you are not careful, you will fall down a precipice, or be overtaken by an avalanche, or the ice will break while you are crossing it. There are a thousand ways in which you might get hurt."

"A man of ready wit with a quick eye," replied Tell complacently, "never gets hurt. The mountain has no terror for her children. I am a child of the mountain."

"You are certainly a child!" snapped Hedwig. "It is no use my arguing with you."

"Not very much," agreed Tell, "for I am just off to the town. I have an appointment with your papa and some other gentlemen."

(I forgot to say so before, but Hedwig was the daughter of Walter Furst.)

"Now, *what* are you and papa plotting?" asked Hedwig. "I know there is something going on. I suspected it when papa brought Werner Stauffacher and the other man here, and you wouldn't let me listen. What is it? Some dangerous scheme, I suppose?"

"Now, how in the world do you get those sort of ideas into your head?" Tell laughed. "Dangerous scheme! As if I should plot dangerous schemes with your papa!"

"I know," said Hedwig. "You can't deceive *me!* There is a plot afoot against the Governor, and you are in it."

"A man must help his country."

"They're sure to place you where there is most danger. I know them. Don't go. Send Walter down with a note to say that you regret that an unfortunate previous engagement, which you have just recollected, will make it impossible for you to accept their kind invitation to plot."

"No; I must go."

"And there is another thing," continued Hedwig: "Gessler the Governor is in the town now."

"He goes away to-day."

"Well, wait till he has gone. You must not meet him. He bears you malice."

"To me his malice cannot do much harm. I do what's right, and fear no enemy."

"Those who do right," said Hedwig, "are those he hates the most. And you know he has never forgiven you for speaking like that when you met him in the ravine. Keep away from the town for to-day. Do anything else. Go hunting, if you will."

"No," said Tell; "I promised. I must go. Come along, Walter."

"You *aren't* going to take that poor *dear* child? Come here, Walter, directly minute!'

"Want to go with father," said Walter, beginning to cry, for his father had promised to take him with him the next time he went to the town, and he had saved his pocket-money for the occasion.

"Oh, let the boy come," said Tell. "William will stay with you, won't you, William?"

"All right, father," said William.

"Well, mark my words," said Hedwig, "if something bad does not happen I shall be surprised."

"Oh no," said Tell. "What can happen?"

And without further delay he set off with Walter for the town.

Chapter 6

In the meantime all kinds of things of which Tell had no suspicion had been happening in the town. The fact that there were no newspapers in Switzerland at that time often made him a little behindhand as regarded the latest events. He had to depend, as a rule, on visits from his friends, who would sit in his kitchen and tell him all about everything that had been going on for the last few days. And, of course, when there was anything very exciting happening in the town, nobody had time to trudge up the hill to Tell's chalet. They all wanted to be in the town enjoying the fun.

What had happened now was this. It was the chief amusement of the Governor, Gessler (who, you will remember, was *not* a nice man), when he had a few moments to spare from the cares of governing, to sit down and think out some new way of annoying the Swiss people. He was one of those persons who

"only do it to annoy,
Because they know it teases."

What he liked chiefly was to forbid something. He would find out what the people most enjoyed doing, and then he would send a herald to say that he was very sorry, but it must stop. He found that this annoyed the Swiss more than anything. But now he was rather puzzled what to do, for he had forbidden everything he could think of. He had forbidden dancing and singing, and playing on any sort of musical instrument, on the ground that these things made such a noise, and disturbed people who wanted to work. He had forbidden the eating of everything except bread and the simplest sorts of meat, because he said that anything else upset people, and made them unfit to do anything except sit still and say how ill they were. And he had forbidden all sorts of games, because he said they were a waste of time.

So that now, though he wanted dreadfully to forbid something else, he could not think of anything.

Then he had an idea, and this was it:

He told his servants to cut a long pole. And they cut a very long pole. Then he said to them, "Go into the hall and bring me one of my hats. Not my best hat, which I wear on Sundays and on State occasions; nor yet my second-best, which I wear every day; nor yet, again, the one I wear when I am out hunting, for all these I need. Fetch me, rather, the oldest of my hats." And they fetched him the very oldest of his hats. Then he said, "Put it on top of the pole." And they put it right on top of the pole. And, last of all, he said, "Go and set up the pole in the middle of the meadow just outside the gates of the town." And they went and set up the pole in the very middle of the meadow just outside the gates of the town.

Then he sent his heralds out to north and south and east and west to summon the people together, because he said he had something very important and special to say to them. And the people came in tens, and fifties, and hundreds, men, women, and children; and they stood waiting in front of the Palace steps till Gessler the Governor should come out and say something very important and special to them.

And punctually at eleven o'clock, Gessler, having finished a capital breakfast, came out on to the top step and spoke to them.

"Ladies and gentlemen," – he began. (A voice from the crowd: "Speak up!")

"Ladies and gentlemen," he began again, in a louder voice, "if I could catch the man who said 'Speak up!' I would have him bitten in the neck by wild elephants. (Applause.) I have called you to this place to-day to explain to you my reason for putting up a pole, on the top of which is one of my caps, in the meadow just outside the city gates. It is this: You all, I know, respect and love me." Here he paused for the audience to cheer, but as they remained quite silent he went on: "You would all, I know, like to come to my Palace every day and do reverence to me. (A voice: 'No, no!') If I could catch the man who said 'No, no!' I would have him stung on the soles of the feet by pink scorpions; and if he was the same man who said 'Speak up!' a little while ago, the number of scorpions should be doubled. (Loud applause.) As I was saying before I was interrupted, I know you would like to come to my Palace and do reverence to me there. But, as you are many and space is limited, I am obliged to refuse you that pleasure. However, being anxious not to disappoint you, I have set up my cap in the meadow, and you may do reverence to *that*. In fact, you *must*. Everybody is to look on that cap as if it were me. (A voice: 'It ain't so ugly as you!') If I could catch the man who made that remark I would have him tied up and teased by trained bluebottles. (Deafening applause.) In fact, to put the matter briefly, if anybody crosses that meadow without bowing down before that cap, my soldiers will arrest him, and I will have him pecked on the nose by infuriated blackbirds. So there! Soldiers, move that crowd on!"

And Gessler disappeared indoors again, just as a volley of eggs and cabbages whistled through the air. And the soldiers began to hustle the crowd down the various streets till the open space in front of the Palace gates was quite cleared of them. All this happened the day before Tell and Walter set out for the town.

CHAPTER 7

HAVING set up the pole and cap in the meadow, Gessler sent two of his bodyguard, Friesshardt (I should think you would be safe in pronouncing this Freeze-hard, but you had better ask somebody who knows) and Leuthold, to keep watch there all day, and see that nobody passed by without kneeling down before the pole and taking off his hat to it.

But the people, who prided themselves on being what they called *uppen zie schnuffen*, or, as we should say, "up to snuff," and equal to every occasion, had already seen a way out of the difficulty. They knew that if they crossed the meadow they must bow down before the pole, which they did not want to do, so it occurred to them that an ingenious way of preventing this would be not to cross the meadow. So they went the long way round, and the two soldiers spent a lonely day.

"What I sez," said Friesshardt, "is, wot's the use of us wasting our time here?" (Friesshardt was not a very well-educated man, and he did not speak good grammar.) "None of these here people ain't a-going to bow down to that there hat. Of course they ain't. Why, I can remember the time when this meadow was like a fair – everybody a-shoving and a-jostling one another for elbow-room; and look at it now! It's a desert. That's what it is, a desert. What's the good of us wasting of our time here, I sez. That's what I sez.

"And they're artful, too, mind yer," he continued. "Why, only this morning, I sez to myself, 'Friesshardt,' I sez, 'you just wait till twelve o'clock,' I sez, "cos that's when they leave the council-house, and then they'll *have* to cross the meadow. And then we'll see what we *shall* see,' I sez. Like that, I sez. Bitter-like, yer know. 'We'll see,' I sez, 'what we *shall* see.' So I waited, and at twelve o'clock out they came, dozens of them, and began to cross the meadow. 'And now,' sez I to myself, 'look out for larks.' But what happened? Why, when they came to the pole, the priest stood in front of it, and the sacristan rang the bell, and they all fell down on their knees. But they were saying their prayers, not doing obeisance to the hat. That's what *they* were doing. Artful – that's what *they* are!"

And Friesshardt kicked the foot of the pole viciously with his iron boot.

"It's my belief," said Leuthold (Leuthold is the thin soldier you see in the picture) – "it's my firm belief that they are laughing at us. There! Listen to that!"

A voice made itself heard from behind a rock not far off.

"Where did you get that hat?" said the voice.

"There!" grumbled Leuthold; "they're always at it. Last time it was, 'Who's your hatter?' Why, we're the laughing-stock of the place. We're like two rogues in a pillory. 'Tis rank disgrace for one who wears a sword to stand as sentry o'er an empty hat. To make obeisance to a hat! I' faith, such a command is downright foolery!"

"Well," said Friesshardt, "and why not bow before an empty hat? Thou hast oft bow'd before an empty skull. Ha, ha! I was always one for a joke, yer know."

"Here come some people," said Leuthold. "At last! And they're only the rabble, after all. You don't catch any of the better sort of people coming here."

A crowd was beginning to collect on the edge of the meadow. Its numbers swelled every minute, until quite a hundred of the commoner sort must have been gathered together. They stood pointing at the pole and talking among themselves, but nobody made any movement to cross the meadow.

At last somebody shouted "Yah!"

The soldiers took no notice.

Somebody else cried "Booh!'"

"Pass along there, pass along!" said the soldiers.

Cries of "Where did you get that hat?" began to come from the body of the crowd. When the Swiss invented a catch-phrase they did not drop it in a hurry.

"Where – did – you – get – that – HAT?" they shouted.

Friesshardt and Leuthold stood like two statues in armour, paying no attention to the remarks of the rabble. This annoyed the rabble. They began to be more personal.

"You in the second-hand lobster-tin," shouted one – he meant

Friesshardt, whose suit of armour, though no longer new, hardly deserved this description – "who's your hatter?"

"Can't yer see," shouted a friend, when Friesshardt made no reply, "the pore thing ain't alive? 'E's stuffed!"

Roars of laughter greeted this sally. Friesshardt, in spite of the fact that he enjoyed a joke, turned pink.

"'E's blushing!" shrieked a voice.

Friesshardt turned purple.

Then things got still more exciting.

"'Ere," said a rough voice in the crowd impatiently, "wot's the good of *torkin'* to 'em? Gimme that 'ere egg, missus!"

And in another instant an egg flew across the meadow, and burst over Leuthold's shoulder. The crowd howled with delight. This was something *like* fun, thought they, and the next moment eggs, cab-

bages, cats, and missiles of every sort darkened the air. The two soldiers raved and shouted, but did not dare to leave their post. At last,
just as the storm was at its height, it ceased, as if by magic. Everyone
in the crowd turned round, and, as he turned, jumped into the air
and waved his hat.

A deafening cheer went up.

"Hurrah!" cried the mob; "here comes good old Tell! *Now* there's
going to be a jolly row!"

CHAPTER 8

TELL came striding along, Walter by his side, and his cross-bow over
his shoulder. He knew nothing about the hat having been placed on
the pole, and he was surprised to see such a large crowd gathered
in the meadow. He bowed to the crowd in his polite way, and the
crowd gave three cheers and one more, and he bowed again.

"Hullo!" said Walter suddenly; "look at that hat up there, father.
On the pole."

"What is the hat to us?" said Tell; and he began to walk across
the meadow with an air of great dignity, and Walter walked by his
side, trying to look just like him.

"Here! hi!" shouted the soldiers. "Stop! You haven't bowed down
to the cap."

Tell looked scornful, but said nothing. Walter looked still more
scornful.

"Ho, there!" shouted Friesshardt, standing in front of him. "I bid
you stand in the Emperor's name."

"My good fellow," said Tell, "please do not bother me. I am in a
hurry. I really have nothing for you."

"My orders is," said Friesshardt, "to stand in this 'ere meadow
and to see as how all them what passes through it does obeisance to
that there hat. Them's Governor's orders, them is. So now."

"My good fellow," said Tell, "let me pass. I shall get cross, I know
I shall."

Shouts of encouragement from the crowd, who were waiting pa-
tiently for the trouble to begin.

"Go it, Tell!" they cried. "Don't stand talking to him. Hit him
a kick!"

Friesshardt became angrier every minute.

"My orders is," he said again, "to arrest them as don't bow down to the hat, and for two pins, young feller, I'll arrest you. So which is

it to be? Either you bow down to that there hat or you come along of me."

Tell pushed him aside, and walked on with his chin in the air. Walter went with him, with his chin in the air.

WHACK!

A howl of dismay went up from the crowd as they saw Friesshardt raise his pike and bring it down with all his force on Tell's head. The sound of the blow went echoing through the meadow and up the hills and down the valleys.

"Ow!" cried Tell.

"*Now*," thought the crowd, "things must begin to get exciting."

Tell's first idea was that one of the larger mountains in the

neighbourhood had fallen on top of him. Then he thought that there must have been an earthquake. Then it gradually dawned upon him that he had been hit by a mere common soldier with a pike. Then he *was* angry.

"Look here!" he began.

"Look there!" said Friesshardt, pointing to the cap.

"You've hurt my head very much," said Tell. "Feel the bump. If I hadn't happened to have a particularly hard head I don't know what might not have happened;" and he raised his fist and hit Friesshardt; but as Friesshardt was wearing a thick iron helmet the blow did not hurt him very much.

But it had the effect of bringing the crowd to Tell's assistance. They had been waiting all this time for him to begin the fighting, for though they were very anxious to attack the soldiers, they did not like to do so by themselves. They wanted a leader.

So when they saw Tell hit Friesshardt, they tucked up their sleeves, grasped their sticks and cudgels more tightly, and began to run across the meadow towards him.

Neither of the soldiers noticed this. Friesshardt was busy arguing with Tell, and Leuthold was laughing at Friesshardt. So when the people came swarming up with their sticks and cudgels they were taken by surprise. But every soldier in the service of Gessler was as brave as a lion, and Friesshardt and Leuthold were soon hitting back merrily, and making a good many of the crowd wish that they had stayed at home. The two soldiers were wearing armour, of course, so that it was difficult to hurt them; but the crowd, who wore no armour, found that *they* could get hurt very easily. Conrad Hunn, for instance, was attacking Friesshardt, when the soldier happened to drop his pike. It fell on Conrad's toe, and Conrad limped away, feeling that fighting was no fun unless you had thick boots on.

And so for a time the soldiers had the best of the fight.

CHAPTER 9

FOR many minutes the fight raged furiously round the pole, and the earth shook beneath the iron boots of Friesshardt and Leuthold as they rushed about, striking out right and left with their fists and the flats of their pikes. Seppi the cowboy (an ancestor, by the way, of Buffalo Bill) went down before a tremendous blow by Friesshardt, and Leuthold knocked Klaus von der Flue head over heels.

"What you *want*" said Arnold of Sewa, who had seen the beginning of the fight from the window of his cottage and had hurried to join it, and, as usual, to give advice to everybody – "what you want

here is guile. That's what you want – guile, cunning. Not brute force, mind you. It's no good rushing at a man in armour and hitting him. He only hits you back. You should employ guile. Thus. Observe."

He had said these words standing on the outskirts of the crowd. He now grasped his cudgel and began to steal slowly towards Friesshardt, who had just given Werni the huntsman such a hit with his pike that the sound of it was still echoing in the mountains, and was now busily engaged in disposing of Jost Weiler. Arnold of Sewa crept stealthily behind him, and was just about to bring his cudgel down on his head, when Leuthold, catching sight of him, saved his

33

comrade by driving his pike with all his force into Arnold's side. Arnold said afterwards that it completely took his breath away. He rolled over, and after being trodden on by everybody for some minutes, got up and limped back to his cottage, where he went straight to bed, and did not get up for two days.

All this time Tell had been standing a little way off with his arms folded, looking on. While it was a quarrel simply between himself and Friesshardt he did not mind fighting. But when the crowd joined in he felt that it was not fair to help so many men attack one, however badly that one might have behaved.

He now saw that the time had come to put an end to the disturbance. He drew an arrow from his quiver, placed it in his crossbow, and pointed it at the hat. Friesshardt, seeing what he intended to do, uttered a shout of horror and rushed to stop him. But at that moment somebody in the crowd hit him so hard with a spade that his helmet was knocked over his eyes, and before he could raise it again the deed was done. Through the cap and through the pole and out at the other side sped the arrow. And the first thing he saw when he opened his eyes was Tell standing beside him twirling his moustache, while all around the crowd danced and shouted and threw their caps into the air with joy.

"A mere trifle," said Tell modestly.

The crowd cheered again and again.

Friesshardt and Leuthold lay on the ground beside the pole, feeling very sore and bruised, and thought that perhaps, on the whole, they had better stay there. There was no knowing what the crowd might do after this, if they began to fight again. So they lay on the ground and made no attempt to interfere with the popular rejoicings. What they *wanted*, as Arnold of Sewa might have said if he had been there, was a few moments' complete rest. Leuthold's helmet had been hammered with sticks until it was over his eyes and all out of shape, and Friesshardt's was very little better. And they both felt just as if they had been run over in the street by a horse and cart.

"Tell!" shouted the crowd. "Hurrah for Tell! Good old Tell!"

"Tell's the boy!" roared Ulric the smith. "Not another man in Switzerland could have made that shot."

"No," shrieked everybody, "not another!"

"Speech!" cried someone from the edge of the crowd.

"Speech! Speech! Tell, speech!" Everybody took up the cry.

"No, no," said Tell, blushing.

"Go on, go on!" shouted the crowd.

"Oh, I couldn't," said Tell; "I don't know what to say."

"Anything will do. Speech! Speech!"

Ulric the smith and Ruodi the fisherman hoisted Tell on to their shoulders, and, having coughed once or twice, he said:

"Gentlemen – "

Cheers from the crowd.

"Gentlemen," said Tell again, "this is the proudest moment of my life."

35

More cheers.

"I don't know what you want me to talk about. I have never made a speech before. Excuse my emotion. This is the proudest moment of my life. To-day is a great day for Switzerland. We have struck the first blow of the revolution. Let us strike some more."

Shouts of "Hear, hear!" from the crowd, many of whom, misunderstanding Tell's last remark, proceeded to hit Leuthold and Friesshardt, until stopped by cries of "Order!" from Ulric the smith.

"Gentlemen," continued Tell, "the floodgates of revolution have been opened. From this day they will stalk through the land burning to ashes the slough of oppression which our tyrant Governor has erected in our midst. I have only to add that this is the proudest moment of my life, and – – "

He was interrupted by a frightened voice.

"Look out, you chaps," said the voice; "here comes the Governor!"

Gessler, with a bodyguard of armed men, had entered the meadow, and was galloping towards them.

CHAPTER 10

GESSLER came riding up on his brown horse, and the crowd melted away in all directions, for there was no knowing what the Governor might not do if he found them plotting. They were determined to rebel and to throw off his tyrannous yoke, but they preferred to do it quietly and comfortably, when he was nowhere near.

So they ran away to the edge of the meadow, and stood there in groups, waiting to see what was going to happen. Not even Ulric the smith and Ruodi the fisherman waited, though they knew quite well that Tell had not nearly finished his speech. They set the orator down, and began to walk away, trying to look as if they had been doing nothing in particular, and were going to go on doing it – only somewhere else.

Tell was left standing alone in the middle of the meadow by the pole. He scorned to run away like the others, but he did not at all like the look of things. Gessler was a stern man, quick to punish any insult, and there were two of his soldiers lying on the ground with their nice armour all spoiled and dented, and his own cap on top of the pole had an arrow right through the middle of it, and would never look the same again, however much it might be patched. It seemed to Tell that there was a bad time coming.

Gessler rode up, and reined in his horse.

"Now then, now then, now then!" he said, in his quick, abrupt

way. "What's this? what's this? what's this?"

(When a man repeats what he says three times, you can see that he is not in a good temper.)

Friesshardt and Leuthold got up, saluted, and limped slowly towards him. They halted beside his horse, and stood to attention. The tears trickled down their cheeks.

"Come, come, come!" said Gessler; "tell me all about it."

And he patted Friesshardt on the head. Friesshardt bellowed.

Gessler beckoned to one of his courtiers.

"Have you a handkerchief?" he said.

"I have a handkerchief, your Excellency."

"Then dry this man's eyes."

The courtier did as he was bidden.

"*Now*," said Gessler, when the drying was done, and Friesshardt's tears had ceased, "what has been happening here? I heard a cry of 'Help!' as I came up. Who cried 'Help!'?"

"Please, your lordship's noble Excellencyship," said Friesshardt, "it was me, Friesshardt."

"You should say, 'It was I,'" said Gessler. "Proceed."

"Which I am a loyal servant of your Excellency's, and in your Excellency's army, and seeing as how I was told to stand by this 'ere pole and guard that there hat, I stood by this 'ere pole, and guarded that there hat – all day, I did, your Excellency. And then up comes this man here, and I says to him – 'Bow down to the hat,' I says. 'Ho!' he says to me – 'ho, indeed!' and he passed on without so much as nodding. So I takes my pike, and I taps him on the head to remind him, as you may say, that there was something he was forgetting, and he ups and hits me, he does. And then the crowd runs up with their sticks and hits me and Leuthold cruel, your Excellency. And while we was a-fighting with them, this here man I'm a-telling you about, your Excellency, he outs with an arrow, puts it into his bow, and sends it through the hat, and I don't see how you'll ever be able to wear it again. It's a waste of a good hat, your Excellency – that's what it is. And then the people, they puts me and Leuthold on the ground, and hoists this here man – Tell, they call him – up on their shoulders, and he starts making a speech, when up you comes, your Excellency. That's how it all was."

Gessler turned pale with rage, and glared fiercely at Tell, who stood before him in the grasp of two of the bodyguard.

"Ah," he said, "Tell, is it? Good-day to you, Tell. I think we've met before, Tell? Eh, Tell?"

"We have, your Excellency. It was in the ravine of Schachenthal," said Tell firmly.

"Your memory is good, Tell. So is mine. I think you made a few remarks to me on that occasion, Tell – a few chatty remarks? Eh, Tell?"

"Very possibly, your Excellency."

"You were hardly polite, Tell."

"If I offended you I am sorry."

"I am glad to hear it, Tell. I think you will be even sorrier before long. So you've been ill-treating my soldiers, eh?"

"It was not I who touched them."

"Oh, so you didn't touch them? Ah! But you defied my power by refusing to bow down to the hat. I set up that hat to prove the people's loyalty. I am afraid you are not loyal, Tell."

"I was a little thoughtless, not disloyal. I passed the hat without thinking."

"You should always think, Tell. It is very dangerous not to do so. And I suppose that you shot your arrow through the hat without thinking?"

"I was a little carried away by excitement, your Excellency."

"Dear, dear! Carried away by excitement, were you? You must really be more careful, Tell. One of these days you will be getting yourself into trouble. But it seems to have been a very fine shot. You *are* a capital marksman, I believe?"

"Father's the best shot in all Switzerland," piped a youthful voice. "He can hit an apple on a tree a hundred yards away. I've seen him. Can't you, father?"

Walter, who had run away when the fighting began, had returned on seeing his father in the hands of the soldiers.

Gessler turned a cold eye upon him.

"Who is this?" he asked.

CHAPTER 11

"IT is my son Walter, your Excellency," said Tell.

"Your son? Indeed. This is very interesting. Have you any more children?"

"I have one other boy."

"And which of them do you love the most, eh?"

"I love them both alike, your Excellency."

"Dear me! Quite a happy family. Now, listen to me, Tell. I know you are fond of excitement, so I am going to try to give you a little. Your son says that you can hit an apple on a tree a hundred yards away, and I am sure you have every right to be very proud of such a feat. Friesshardt!"

"Your Excellency?"

"Bring me an apple."

Friesshardt picked one up. Some apples had been thrown at him and Leuthold earlier in the day, and there were several lying about.

"Which I'm afraid as how it's a little bruised, your Excellency," he said, "having hit me on the helmet."

"Thank you. I do not require it for eating purposes," said Gessler. "Now, Tell, I have here an apple – a simple apple, not over-ripe. I should like to test that feat of yours. So take your bow – I see you have it in your hand – and get ready to shoot. I am going to put this apple on your son's head. He will be placed a hundred yards away from you, and if you do not hit the apple with your first shot your life shall pay forfeit."

And he regarded Tell with a look of malicious triumph.

"Your Excellency, it cannot be!" cried Tell; "the thing is too monstrous. Perhaps your Excellency is pleased to jest. You cannot bid a father shoot an apple from off his son's head! Consider, your Excellency!"

"You shall shoot the apple from off the head of this boy," said Gessler sternly. "I do not jest. That is my will."

"Sooner would I die," said Tell.

"If you do not shoot you die with the boy. Come, come, Tell, why so cautious? They always told me that you loved perilous enterprises, and yet when I give you one you complain. I could understand anybody else shrinking from the feat. But you! Hitting apples at a hundred yards is child's play to you. And what does it matter where the apple is – whether it is on a tree or on a boy's head? It is an apple just the same. Proceed, Tell."

The crowd, seeing a discussion going on, had left the edge of the meadow and clustered round to listen. A groan of dismay went up at the Governor's words.

"Down on your knees, boy," whispered Rudolph der Harras to Walter – "down on your knees, and beg his Excellency for your life."

"I won't!" said Walter stoutly.

"Come," said Gessler, "clear a path there – clear a path! Hurry yourselves. I won't have this loitering. Look you, Tell: attend to me for a moment. I find you in the middle of this meadow deliberately defying my authority and making sport of my orders. I find you in the act of stirring up discontent among my people with speeches. I might have you executed without ceremony. But do I? No. Nobody shall say that Hermann Gessler the Governor is not kind-hearted. I say to myself, 'I will give this man one chance.' I place your fate in your own skilful hands. How can a man complain of harsh treatment when he is made master of his own fate? Besides, I don't ask you to do anything difficult. I merely bid you perform what must be to you a simple shot. You boast of your unerring aim. Now is the time to prove it. Clear the way there!"

Walter Furst flung himself on his knees before the Governor.

"Your Highness," he cried, "none deny your power. Let it be mingled with mercy. It is excellent, as an English poet will say in a few hundred years, to have a giant's strength, but it is tyrannous to use it like a giant. Take the half of my possessions, but spare my son-in-law."

But Walter Tell broke in impatiently, and bade his grandfather rise, and not kneel to the tyrant.

"Where must I stand?" asked he. "I'm not afraid. Father can hit a bird upon the wing."

"You see that lime-tree yonder," said Gessler to his soldiers; "take the boy and bind him to it."

"I will not be bound!" cried Walter. "I am not afraid. I'll stand still. I won't breathe. If you bind me I'll kick!"

"Let us bind your eyes, at least," said Rudolph der Harras.

"Do you think I fear to see father shoot?" said Walter. "I won't stir an eyelash. Father, show the tyrant how you can shoot. He thinks you're going to miss. Isn't he an old donkey!"

"Very well, young man," muttered Gessler, "we'll see who is laughing five minutes from now." And once more he bade the crowd stand back and leave a way clear for Tell to shoot.

CHAPTER 12

THE crowd fell back, leaving a lane down which Walter walked, carrying the apple. There was dead silence as he passed. Then the people began to whisper excitedly to one another.

"Shall this be done before our eyes?" said Arnold of Melchthal to Werner Stauffacher. "Of what use was it that we swore an oath to rebel if we permit this? Let us rise and slay the tyrant."

Werner Stauffacher, prudent man, scratched his chin thoughtfully.

"We-e-ll," he said, "you see, the difficulty is that we are not armed and the soldiers *are*. There is nothing I should enjoy more than slaying the tyrant, only I have an idea that the tyrant would slay us. You see my point?"

"Why were we so slow!" groaned Arnold. "We should have risen before, and then this would never have happened. Who was it that advised us to delay?"

"We-e-ll," said Stauffacher (who had himself advised delay), "I can't quite remember at the moment, but I dare say you could find out by looking up the minutes of our last meeting. I know the motion was carried by a majority of two votes. See! Gessler grows impatient."

Gessler, who had been fidgeting on his horse for some time, now spoke again, urging Tell to hurry.

"Begin!" he cried – "begin!"

"Immediately," replied Tell, fitting the arrow to the string.

Gessler began to mock him once more.

"You see now," he said, "the danger of carrying arms. I don't know if you have ever noticed it, but arrows very often recoil on the man who carries them. The only man who has any business to possess a weapon is the ruler of a country – myself, for instance. A low, common fellow – if you will excuse the description – like yourself only grows proud through being armed, and so offends those above him. But, of course, it's no business of mine. I am only telling you what I think about it. Personally, I like to encourage my subjects to shoot; that is why I am giving you such a splendid mark to shoot at. You see, Tell?"

Tell did not reply. He raised his bow and pointed it. There was a stir of excitement in the crowd, more particularly in that part of the crowd which stood on his right, for, his hand trembling for the first time in his life, Tell had pointed his arrow, not at his son, but straight into the heart of the crowd.

"Here! Hi! That's the wrong way! More to the left!" shouted the people in a panic, while Gessler roared with laughter, and bade Tell shoot and chance it.

"If you can't hit the apple or your son," he chuckled, "you can bring down one of your dear fellow-countrymen."

Tell lowered his bow, and a sigh of relief went through the crowd.

"My eyes are swimming," he said; "I cannot see."

Then he turned to the Governor.

"I cannot shoot," he said; "bid your soldiers kill me."

"No," said Gessler – "no, Tell. That is not at all what I want. If I had wished my soldiers to kill you, I should not have waited for a formal invitation from you. I have no desire to see you slain. Not at present. I wish to see you shoot. Come, Tell, they say you can do everything, and are afraid of nothing. Only the other day, I hear, you carried a man, one Baumgartner – that was his name, I think – across a rough sea in an open boat. You may remember it? I particularly wished to catch Baumgartner, Tell. Now, this is a feat which calls for much less courage. Simply to shoot an apple off a boy's head. A child could do it."

While he was speaking, Tell had been standing in silence, his hands trembling and his eyes fixed, sometimes on the Governor, sometimes on the sky. He now seized his quiver, and taking from it a second arrow, placed it in his belt. Gessler watched him, but said nothing.

"Shoot, father!" cried Walter from the other end of the lane; "I'm not afraid."

45

Tell, calm again now, raised his bow and took a steady aim. Everybody craned forward, the front ranks in vain telling those behind that there was nothing to be gained by pushing. Gessler bent over his horse's neck and peered eagerly towards Walter. A great hush fell on all as Tell released the string.

"Phut!" went the string, and the arrow rushed through the air.

A moment's suspense, and then a terrific cheer rose from the spectators.

The apple had leaped from Walter's head, pierced through the centre.

Chapter 13

Intense excitement instantly reigned. Their suspense over, the crowd cheered again and again, shook hands with one another, and flung their caps into the air. Everyone was delighted, for everyone was fond of Tell and Walter. It also pleased them to see the Governor disappointed. He had had things his own way for so long that it was a pleasant change to see him baffled in this manner. Not since Switzerland became a nation had the meadow outside the city gates been the scene of such rejoicings.

Walter had picked up the apple with the arrow piercing it, and was showing it proudly to all his friends.

"I told you so," he kept saying; "I knew father wouldn't hurt me. Father's the best shot in all Switzerland."

"That was indeed a shot!" exclaimed Ulric the smith; "it will ring through the ages. While the mountains stand will the tale of Tell the bowman be told."

Rudolph der Harras took the apple from Walter and showed it to Gessler, who had been sitting transfixed on his horse.

"See," he said, "the arrow has passed through the very centre. It was a master shot."

"It was very nearly a 'Master Walter shot,'" said Rosselmann the priest severely, fixing the Governor with a stern eye.

Gessler made no answer. He sat looking moodily at Tell, who had dropped his cross-bow and was standing motionless, still gazing in the direction in which the arrow had sped. Nobody liked to be the first to speak to him.

"Well," said Rudolph der Harras, breaking an awkward silence, "I suppose it's all over now? May as well be moving, eh?"

He bit a large piece out of the apple, which he still held. Walter uttered a piercing scream as he saw the mouthful disappear. Up till now he had shown no signs of dismay, in spite of the peril which he had had to face; but when he watched Rudolph eating the apple, which he naturally looked upon as his own property, he could not keep quiet any longer. Rudolph handed him the apple with an apology, and he began to munch it contentedly.

"Come with me to your mother, my boy," said Rosselmann.

Walter took no notice, but went on eating the apple.

Tell came to himself with a start, looked round for Walter, and began to lead him away in the direction of his home, deaf to all the cheering that was going on around him.

Gessler leaned forward in his saddle.

"Tell," he said, "a word with you."

Tell came back.

"Your Excellency?"

"Before you go I wish you to explain one thing."

"A thousand, your Excellency."

"No, only one. When you were getting ready to shoot at the apple you placed an arrow in the string and a second arrow in your belt."

"A second arrow!" Tell pretended to be very much astonished, but the pretence did not deceive the Governor.

"Yes, a second arrow. Why was that? What did you intend to do with that arrow, Tell?"

Tell looked down uneasily, and twisted his bow about in his hands.

"My lord," he said at last, "it is a bowman's custom. All archers place a second arrow in their belt."

"No, Tell," said Gessler, "I cannot take that answer as the truth. I know there was some other meaning in what you did. Tell me the reason without concealment. Why was it? Your life is safe, whatever it was, so speak out. Why did you take out that second arrow?"

Tell stopped fidgeting with his bow, and met the Governor's eye with a steady gaze.

"Since you promise me my life, your Excellency," he replied, drawing himself up, "I will tell you."

He drew the arrow from his belt and held it up.

The crowd pressed forward, hanging on his words.

"Had my first arrow," said Tell slowly, "pierced my child and not the apple, this would have pierced you, my lord. Had I missed with my first shot, be sure, my lord, that my second would have found its mark."

A murmur of approval broke from the crowd as Tell thrust the arrow back into the quiver and faced the Governor with folded arms and burning eyes. Gessler turned white with fury.

"Seize that man!" he shouted.

My lord, bethink you," whispered Rudolph der Harras; "you promised him his life. Tell, fly!" he cried.

Tell did not move.

"Seize that man and bind him," roared Gessler once more. "If he resists, cut him down."

"I shall not resist," said Tell scornfully. "I should have known the

folly of trusting to a tyrant to keep his word. My death will at least show my countrymen the worth of their Governor's promises."

"Not so," replied Gessler; "no man shall say I ever broke my knightly word. I promised you your life, and I will give you your life. But you are a dangerous man, Tell, and against such must I guard myself. You have told me your murderous purpose. I must look to it that that purpose is not fulfilled. Life I promised you, and life I will give you. But of freedom I said nothing. In my castle at Kussnacht there are dungeons where no ray of sun or moon ever falls. Chained hand and foot in one of these, you will hardly aim your arrows at me. It is rash, Tell, to threaten those who have power over you. Soldiers, bind him and lead him to my ship. I will follow, and will myself conduct him to Kussnacht."

The soldiers tied Tell's hands. He offered no resistance. And amidst the groans of the people he was led away to the shore of the lake, where Gessler's ship lay at anchor.

"Our last chance is gone," said the people to one another. "Where shall we look now for a leader?"

Chapter 14

The castle of Kussnacht lay on the opposite side of the lake, a mighty mass of stone reared on a mightier crag rising sheer out of the waves, which boiled and foamed about its foot. Steep rocks of fantastic shape hemmed it in, and many were the vessels which perished on these, driven thither by the frequent storms that swept over the lake.

Gessler and his men, Tell in their midst, bound and unarmed, embarked early in the afternoon at Fluelen, which was the name of the harbour where the Governor's ship had been moored. Fluelen was about two miles from Kussnacht.

When they had arrived at the vessel they went on board, and Tell was placed at the bottom of the hold. It was pitch dark, and rats scampered over his body as he lay. The ropes were cast off, the sails filled, and the ship made her way across the lake, aided by a favouring breeze.

A large number of the Swiss people had followed Tell and his captors to the harbour, and stood gazing sorrowfully after the ship as it diminished in the distance. There had been whispers of an attempted rescue, but nobody had dared to begin it, and the whispers had led to nothing. Few of the people carried weapons, and the soldiers were clad in armour, and each bore a long pike or a sharp sword. As Arnold of Sewa would have said if he had been present, what the people wanted was prudence. It was useless to attack men so thoroughly able to defend themselves.

Therefore the people looked on and groaned, but did nothing.

For some time the ship sped easily on her way and through a calm sea. Tell lay below, listening to the trampling of the sailors overhead, as they ran about the deck, and gave up all hope of ever seeing his home and his friends again.

But soon he began to notice that the ship was rolling and pitching more than it had been doing at first, and it was not long before he realized that a very violent storm had begun. Storms sprung up very suddenly on the lake, and made it unsafe for boats that attempted to cross it. Often the sea was quite unruffled at the beginning of the crossing, and was rough enough at the end to wreck the largest ship.

Tell welcomed the storm. He had no wish to live if life meant years of imprisonment in a dark dungeon of Castle Kussnacht. Drowning would be a pleasant fate compared with that. He lay at the bottom of the ship, hoping that the next wave would dash them on to a rock and send them to the bottom of the lake. The tossing became worse and worse.

Upon the deck Gessler was standing beside the helmsman, and gazing anxiously across the waters at the rocks that fringed the narrow entrance to the bay a few hundred yards to the east of Castle Kussnacht. This bay was the only spot for miles along the shore at which it was possible to land safely. For miles on either side the coast was studded with great rocks, which would have dashed a ship to pieces in a moment. It was to this bay that Gessler wished to direct the ship. But the helmsman told him that he could not make sure of finding the entrance, so great was the cloud of spray which covered it. A mistake would mean shipwreck.

"My lord," said the helmsman, "I have neither strength nor skill to guide the helm. I do not know which way to turn."

"What are we to do?" asked Rudolph der Harras, who was standing near.

The helmsman hesitated. Then he spoke, eyeing the Governor uneasily.

"Tell could steer us through," he said, "if your lordship would but give him the helm."

Gessler started.

"Tell!" he muttered. "Tell!"

The ship drew nearer to the rocks.

"Bring him here," said Gessler.

Two soldiers went down to the hold and released Tell. They bade him get up and come with them. Tell followed them on deck, and stood before the Governor.

"Tell," said Gessler.

Tell looked at him without speaking.

"Take the helm, Tell," said Gessler, "and steer the ship through those rocks into the bay beyond, or instant death shall be your lot."

Without a word Tell took the helmsman's place, peering keenly into the cloud of foam before him. To right and to left he turned the vessel's head, and to right again, into the very heart of the spray. They were right among the rocks now, but the ship did not strike on them. Quivering and pitching, she was hurried along, until of a sudden the spray-cloud was behind her, and in front the calm waters of the bay.

Gessler beckoned to the helmsman.

"Take the helm again," he said.

He pointed to Tell.

"Bind him," he said to the soldiers.

The soldiers advanced slowly, for they were loath to bind the man who had just saved them from destruction. But the Governor's orders must he obeyed, so they came towards Tell, carrying ropes with which to bind him.

Tell moved a step back. The ship was gliding past a lofty rock. It was such a rock as Tell had often climbed when hunting the chamois. He acted with the quickness of the hunter. Snatching up the bow and quiver which lay on the deck, he sprang on to the bulwark of the vessel, and, with a mighty leap, gained the rock. Another instant, and he was out of reach.

Gessler roared to his bowmen.

"Shoot! shoot!" he cried.

The bowmen hastily fitted arrow to string. They were too late. Tell was ready before them. There was a hiss as the shaft rushed through the air, and the next moment Gessler the Governor fell dead on the deck, pierced through the heart.

Tell's second arrow had found its mark, as his first had done.

CHAPTER 15

THERE is not much more of the story of William Tell. The death of Gessler was a signal to the Swiss to rise in revolt, and soon the whole country was up in arms against the Austrians. It had been chiefly the fear of the Governor that had prevented a rising before. It had been brewing for a long time. The people had been bound by a solemn oath to drive the enemy out of the country. All through Switzerland preparations for a revolution were going on, and nobles and peasants had united.

Directly the news arrived that the Governor was slain, meetings of the people were held in every town in Switzerland, and it was resolved to begin the revolution without delay. All the fortresses that Gessler had built during his years of rule were carried by assault on the same night. The last to fall was one which had only been begun a short time back, and the people who had been forced to help to build it spent a very pleasant hour pulling down the stones which had cost them such labour to put in their place. Even the children helped. It was a great treat to them to break what they pleased without being told not to.

"See," said Tell, as he watched them, "in years to come, when these same children are gray-haired, they will remember this night as freshly as they will remember it to-morrow."

A number of people rushed up, bearing the pole which Gessler's soldiers had set up in the meadow. The hat was still on top of it, nailed to the wood by Tell's arrow.

"Here's the hat!" shouted Ruodi – "the hat to which we were to bow!"

"What shall we do with it?" cried several voices.

"Destroy it! Burn it!" said others. "To the flames with this emblem of tyranny!"

But Tell stopped them.

"Let us preserve it," he said. "Gessler set it up to be a means of enslaving the country; we will set it up as a memorial of our newly-gained liberty. Nobly is fulfilled the oath we swore to drive the tyrants from our land. Let the pole mark the spot where the revolution finished."

"But *is* it finished?" said Arnold of Melchthal. "It is a nice point. When the Emperor of Austria hears that we have killed his friend Gessler, and burnt down all his fine new fortresses, will he not come here to seek revenge?"

"He will," said Tell. "And let him come. And let him bring all his mighty armies. We have driven out the enemy that was in our land. We will meet and drive away the enemy that comes from another country. Switzerland is not easy to attack. There are but a few mountain passes by which the foe can approach. We will stop these with our bodies. And one great strength we have: we are united. And united we need fear no foe."

"Hurrah!" shouted everybody.

"But who is this that approaches?" said Tell. "He seems excited. Perhaps he brings news."

It was Rosselmann the pastor, and he brought stirring news.

"These are strange times in which we live," said Rosselmann, coming up.

"Why, what has happened?" cried everybody.

"Listen, and be amazed."

"Why, what's the matter?"

"The Emperor – – "

"Yes?"

"The Emperor is dead."

"What! dead?"

"Dead!"

"Impossible! How came you by the news?"

"John Muller of Schaffhausen brought it. And he is a truthful man."

"But how did it happen?"

"As the Emperor rode from Stein to Baden the lords of Eschenbach and Tegerfelden, jealous, it is said, of his power, fell upon him with their spears. His bodyguard were on the other side of a stream – the Emperor had just crossed it – and could not come to his assistance. He died instantly."

By the death of the Emperor the revolution in Switzerland was enabled to proceed without check. The successor of the Emperor had too much to do in defending himself against the slayers of his father to think of attacking the Swiss, and by the time he was at leisure they were too strong to be attacked. So the Swiss became free.

As for William Tell, he retired to his home, and lived there very happily ever afterwards with his wife and his two sons, who in a few years became very nearly as skilful in the use of the cross-bow as their father.

Epilogue.

Some say the tale related here
Is amplified and twisted;
Some say it isn't very clear
That William Tell existed;
Some say he freed his country so,
The Governor demolished.
Perhaps he did. I only know
That taxes aren't abolished!

THE ILLUSTRATIONS & ACCOMPANYING DESCRIPTIVE VERSES

PROLOGUE

The Swiss, against their Austrian foes,
Had ne'er a soul to lead 'em,
Till Tell, as you've heard tell, arose
And guided them to freedom.
Tell's tale we tell again – an act
For which pray no one scold us –
This tale of Tell we tell, in fact,
As this Tell tale was told us.

GESSLER'S METHODS OF PERSUASION

Beneath a tyrant foreign yoke,
How love of freedom waxes!
(Especially when foreign folk
Come round collecting taxes.)
The Swiss, held down by Gessler's fist,
Would fain have used evasion;
Yet none there seemed who could resist
His methods of persuasion.

THEY WOULD MARCH ABOUT, BEATING TIN CANS AND SHOUTING

And pride so filled this Gessler's soul
(A monarch's pride outclassing),
He stuck his hat up on a pole,
That all might bow in passing.
Then rose the patriot, William Tell—
"We've groaned 'neath Austria's sway first;
Must we be ruled by poles as well?
I've just a word to say first!"

AN EGG FLEW ACROSS THE MEADOW, AND BURST
OVER LEUTHOLD'S SHOULDER

The crowd about the pole at morn
Used various "persuaders"—
They flung old cans (to prove their scorn
Of all tin-pot invaders);
And cabbage-stumps were freely dealt,
And apples (inexpensive),
And rotten eggs (to show they felt
A foreign yoke offensive).

"HERE! HI!" SHOUTED THE SOLDIERS, "STOP!"

Said William Tell, "And has this cuss
For conquest such a passion
He needs must set his cap at us
In this exalted fashion?"
And then the people gave a cry,
'Twixt joy and apprehension,
To see him pass the symbol by
With studied inattention!

THEY SAW FRIESSHARDT RAISE HIS PIKE, AND BRING IT DOWN WITH ALL
HIS FORCE ON TELL'S HEAD

At first the sentinel, aghast,
Glared like an angry dumb thing;
Then "Hi!" he shouted, "not so fast,
You're overlooking something!"
The sturdy Tell made no response;
Then through the hills resounded
A mighty thwack upon his sconce—
The people were astounded.

"LOOK HERE!" HE BEGAN. "LOOK THERE!" SAID FRIESSHARDT

Could Tell an insult such as this
Ignore or pass? I doubt it!
No, no; that patriotic Swiss
Was very cross about it.
The people, interested now,
Exclaimed, "Here! Stop a minute
If there's to be a jolly row,
By Jingo! we'll be in it!"

Friesshardt Rushed to Stop Him

Said Tell, "This satrap of the Duke
Is sore in need of gumption;
With my good bow I will rebuke
Such arrow-gant presumption."
"Stand back!" the soldier says, says he;
"This roughness is unseemly!"
The people cried, "We will be FREE!"
And so they were – extremely!

THE CROWD DANCED AND SHOUTED

They dealt that soldier thump on thump
(He hadn't any notion,
When on Tell's head he raised that bump,
Of raising this commotion);
Tell's arrow sped, the people crowed,
And loudly cheered his action;
While Tell's expressive features showed
A certain satisfaction.

"Come, Come, Come!" Said Gessler, "Tell Me All About It"

Now, when the cat's away, the mice
Are very enterprising,
But cats return, and, in a trice—
Well, Gessler nipped that rising.
And when those soldiers lodged complaint
(Which truly didn't lack ground),
The people practised self-restraint
And fell into the background.

"I Have Here an Apple"

And Tell, before the tyrant hailed,
No patriot you'd have guessed him,
For even his stout bosom quailed
When Gessler thus addressed him:—
"As you're the crack shot of these Swiss
(I've often heard it said so),
Suppose you take a shot at this,
Placed on your youngster's head – so!"

THERE WAS A STIR OF EXCITEMENT IN THE CROWD

"The bearing," as they say, "of that
Lay in the apple-cation,"
And nobody will wonder at
A parent's agitation;
That anguish filled Tell's bosom proud
Needs scarcely to be stated,
And, it will be observed, the crowd
Was also agitated.

A Moment's Suspense, and Then a Terrific Cheer Arose
From the Spectators

Said Gessler, "This is all my eye!
  Come, hurry up and buck up!
Remember, if you miss, you die—
  That ought to keep your pluck up.
The flying arrow may, no doubt,
  Your offspring's bosom enter – "
But here there rose a mighty shout:
  "By George! He's scored a centre!"

"Seize That Man!" He Shouted

But, as the arrow cleft the core,
Cried G. with indignation,
"What was the second arrow for?
Come, no e-quiver-cation!
You had a second in your fist."
Said Tell, the missile grippin',
"This shaft (had I that apple missed)
Was meant for you, my pippin!"

HE WAS LED AWAY TO THE SHORE OF THE LAKE

With rage the tyrant said, said he,
"It's time to stop this prating;
I find your style of repartee
Extremely irritating.
You'll hang for this, be pleased to note."
On this they bound and gagged him
(For Gessler's castle booked by boat),
And through the village dragged him.

TELL'S SECOND ARROW HAD FOUND ITS MARK

But slips between the cup and lip,
When least expected, peer through—
A storm arose upon the trip
Which Tell alone could steer through.
Thus, of all hands he quickly got
(As you may see) the upper,
At Gessler took a parting shot,
And hurried home to supper.

Epilogue

Some say the tale related here
Is amplified and twisted;
Some say it isn't very clear
That William Tell existed;
Some say he freed his country so,
The Governor demolished.
Perhaps he did. I only know
That taxes aren't abolished!

www.ManorWodehouse.com

CPSIA information can be obtained at www.ICGtesting.com
Printed in the USA
LVOW011618281212

313627LV00001B/140/A